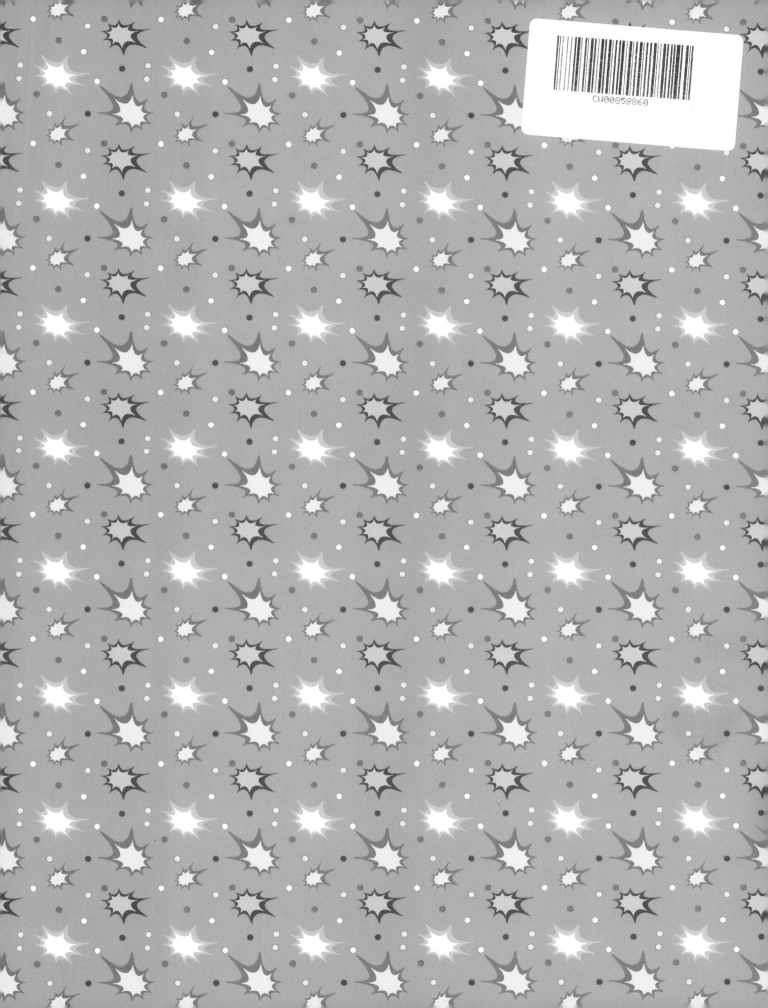

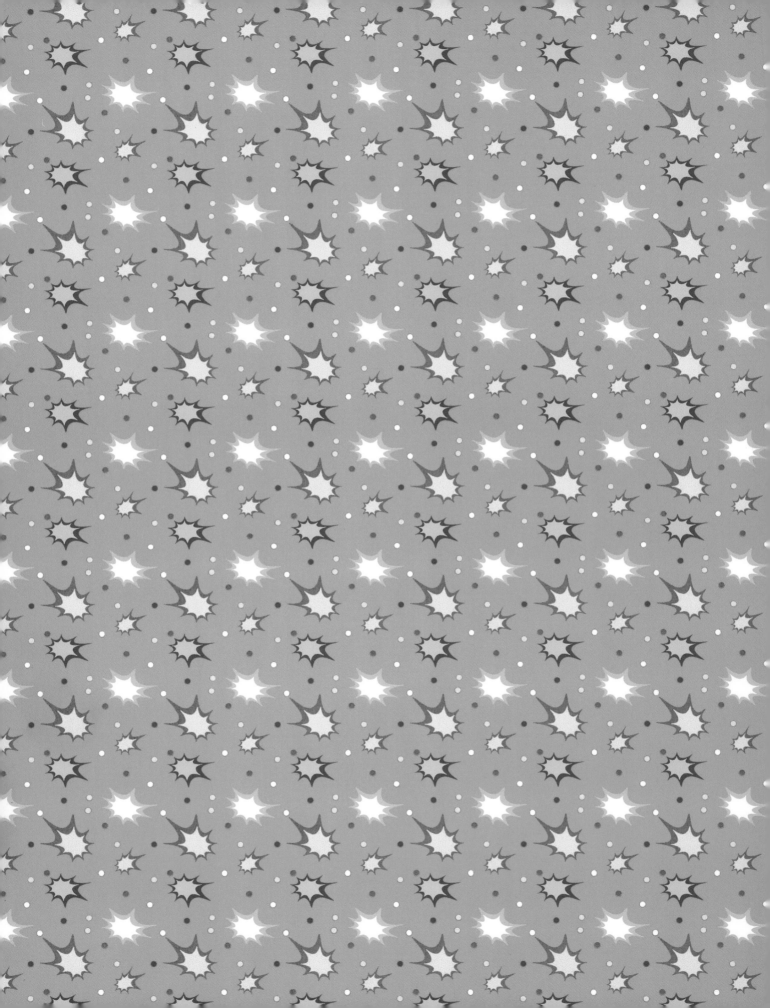

THE SUPER 3
...RESCUE A LION

Written by Sharon Olagunju and illustrated by Tamasin Warnock

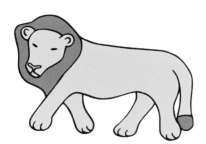

For Zachariah and Asher

GET READY FOR YOUR SUPERHERO ADVENTURE!

MEET OUR HEROES...

X-BOY

X-Boy gets his superhero name from his incredible **X-RAY VISION**! He has **ELASTIC GYMNASTIC MOVES**, and is also a **3D DRAWING EXPERT**. When he's not using his superhero powers, he goes by the name **LITTLE ZEE**.

MECHNO GIRL

Mechno Girl's superhero name comes from her **MECHANICAL ENGINEERING INGENUITY** - she can make a vehicle out of almost anything! But her powers don't stop there; she also has **HYPER-SENSITIVE HEARING** and is **INCREDIBLY STRONG**. People (other than **THE SUPER 3**) know her as **ṢADÉ**.

CHEETECH

You may not be surprised to know that Cheetech gets his superhero name from his **SUPER CHEETAH SPEED**! But what you may not have guessed, is that he's also a **CODING WIZARD** with a **PHOTOGRAPHIC MEMORY**! His other name is **MARLEY**.

SOME USEFUL INFORMATION BEFORE YOU BEGIN...

 Some of our characters may have names that you are unfamiliar with. **TO HELP YOU TO READ ALONG** we have put the correct pronunciations in (brackets).

 In this story our heroes will use some of their powers to solve a problem. **WHEN YOU GET TO PAGE 18**, see if you can guess which **SUPER POWERS** they will use!

 At the end of the story we have included some questions so that you can test out your **SUPER MEMORY**.

 We have also suggested a follow-on activity, so that you can explore your own **SUPERHERO CAPABILITIES**, and your own **SUPER STRENGTHS**.

Little Zee was excited because today was the day that his uncle was coming to visit. He hadn't seen his uncle in almost a year, because he didn't live in England, where Little Zee lived. His uncle lived in a country called Nigeria – which was **VERY** far away. **4,429 MILES** to be precise. And located within the continent of Africa. West Africa – to be even more precise!

"I'm **SO** excited" Little Zee said to his friends, Marley and Ṣadé (Sha-day). "I'm excited because today my uncle Délé (Del-lay) is coming all the way from Nigeria!"

"Where's that?" Marley replied, "It sounds like it's some place **FAR AWAY**."

"**IT IS**" said Ṣadé. "My grandma lives there, and when we went last summer, it took us **NEARLY 7 HOURS** on a plane!"

THE SUPER 3, otherwise known – especially to adults, as Little Zee, Marley and Ṣadé, had been friends pretty much since they were born.

Their mums had been part of the same mum and baby group, and they lived around 10 minutes away from each other's houses.

Today they were at Little Zee's house, because it was the summer holidays, and there was no school. Little Zee's mum had invited Marley and Ṣadé round to play.

THE DOORBELL RANG. It was uncle Délé!
He had arrived from the airport by taxi.

THE SUPER 3 raced downstairs
from Little Zee's bedroom,
to open the door and say hello.

"Well if it isn't the **TERRIFIC TRIO**", uncle Délé said. It was the first time he had met Marley and Ṣadé in person, but he had heard all about their adventures through his brother – Little Zee's dad.

Little Zee loved it when uncle Délé visited. Obviously, he **LOVED** seeing his uncle. But he also **REALLY LOVED** the presents that his uncle always brought with him, any time he paid a visit.

You see, uncle Délé was a **FAMOUS ACTOR** in Nigeria. He worked in 'Nollywood' which is the name of the Nigerian film industry – where around 2,500 films are made **EVERY YEAR**, making it the **SECOND LARGEST** film industry in the world!

It's like Bollywood or Hollywood... You may have heard of them before, or you may have even watched films that have been made there.

Because uncle Délé worked in Nollywood, it meant that whenever he bought Little Zee a present it was an **EXTRA SPECIAL** present. The present was usually bought when he was travelling the world, making films.

Uncle Délé's latest film had been filmed in Kenya, which is in East Africa and is well-known for its safaris.

DO YOU KNOW WHAT A SAFARI IS? A safari is a journey across land that people go on – usually to see and take pictures of wild animals. This happens a lot in parts of Africa because there are places like grasslands, which have **LOADS OF AMAZING ANIMALS** that live there.

Uncle Délé had bought Little Zee a set of handmade animals, that are known to live in the grasslands of Africa. They had been carved out of wood and then painted, which made them **EVEN MORE** special!

The set of animals included a lion, a zebra, a cheetah and a giraffe. Little Zee **LOVED ANIMALS**, and his uncle knew this.

Uncle Délé looked inside his bag. First, he pulled out the cheetah. Next he pulled out the zebra, then the giraffe, then he stopped. "**OH NO**" he gasped in disappointment. **THE SUPER 3** all looked at each other, wondering what he was going to say...

"The lion has **GONE!** I must have forgotten to put it back; I took it out to find my wallet to pay for the cab. Sorry Little Zee, there's not going to be a lion this time. There's no way for me to track down the taxi."

It was at that moment that Little Zee's dad arrived at the door. His uncle very quickly switched his attention to his big brother – forgetting about the lost lion.

So, **THE SUPER 3** headed back upstairs to play.

But Little Zee was upset. Lions were his **FAVOURITE** of all the animals that live in the grasslands.

"Don't be upset" Ṣadé said.
"We can get the lion back."
"**BUT HOW?**" Exclaimed Little Zee.

You see, he had forgotten that when the 3 of them work together to solve a problem, their **SUPER POWERS** come alive!

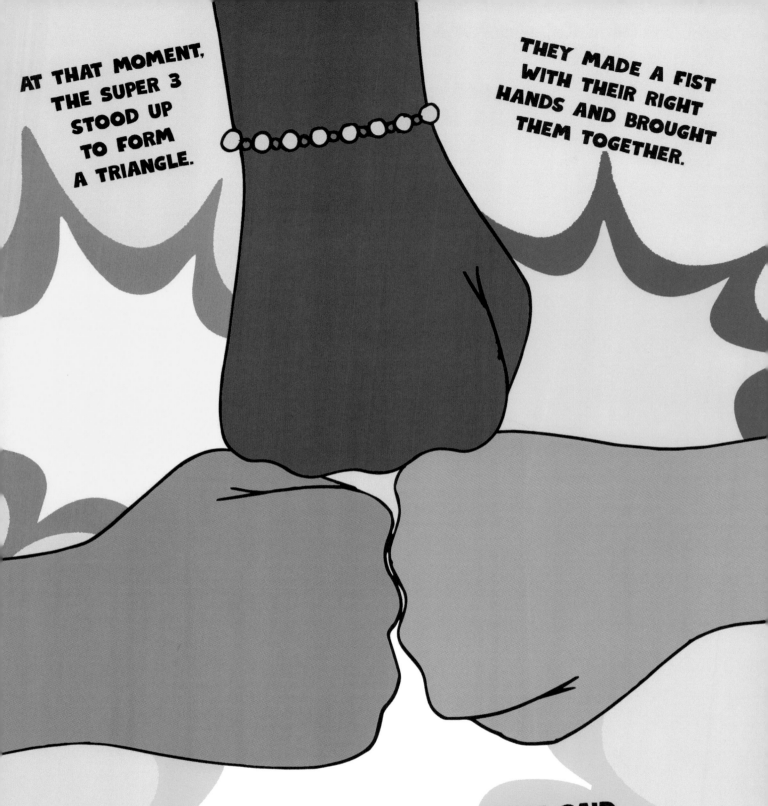

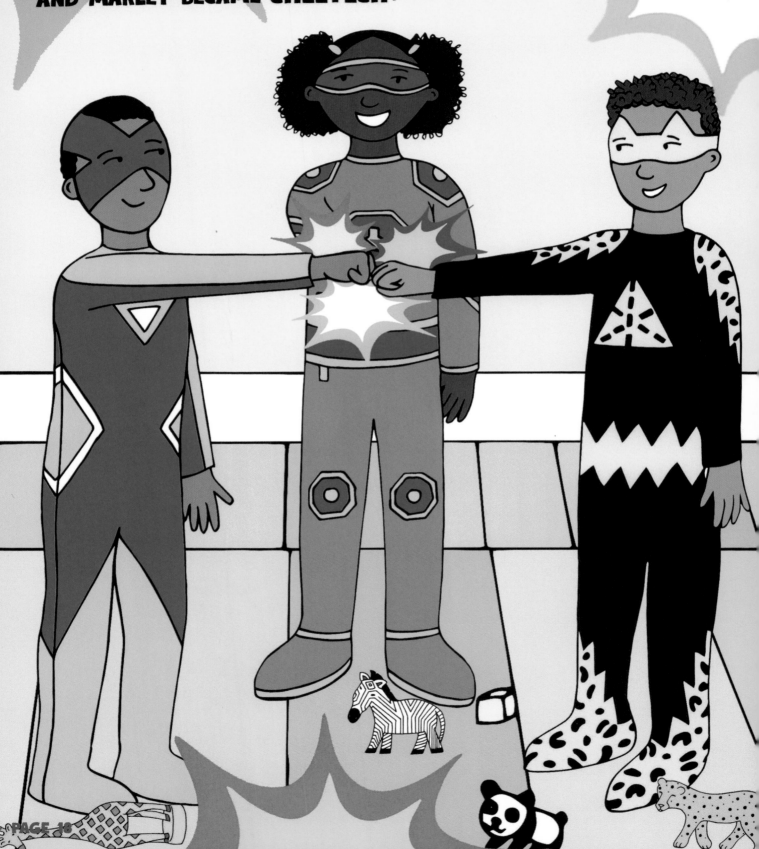

AT THAT MOMENT THEY ALL TRANSFORMED INTO SUPERHEROES!

LITTLE ZEE BECAME X-BOY
ṢADÉ BECAME **MECHNO GIRL**
AND MARLEY BECAME CHEETECH.

CAN YOU GUESS WHICH POWERS OUR HEROES WILL USE TO FIND THE LION?

"RIGHT" said **CHEETECH**. "I have a plan. **MECHNO GIRL**, you need to use your **HYPER-SENSITIVE HEARING** to zone into the sound of the taxi." **CHEETECH** had remembered that when the taxi had dropped off uncle Délé, it had been making a distinctive ticking sound.

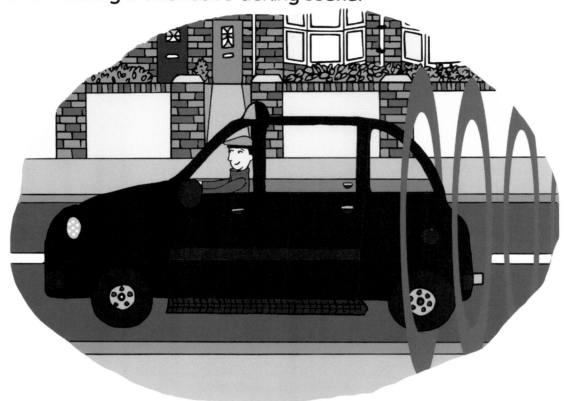

MECHNO GIRL listened intently whilst the others were quiet. **"YES! I'VE GOT IT"** she said excitedly. "It's about two miles away, and it sounds like it's stopped to collect another customer."

"GREAT JOB" shouted **CHEETECH**. They all knew that they only had minutes to get to the taxi, before it drove off for good.

But that was no problem for **CHEETECH**.
With his **SUPER CHEETAH SPEED**, he could catch up
with the car in no time at all.

"**X-BOY**, let's use your mum's old phones and this headset"
CHEETECH said. "Then I can run ahead, whilst you guys direct me to the
exact location of the taxi." And with that, he was gone!

CHEETECH reached the street the taxi was on, within minutes. **THE SUPER 3** used the cameras on the phones, so that they could see where **CHEETECH** was. And it was a good job they did, because when he arrived, there were **TWO TAXIS** on the same street! They were **BOTH** picking people up and **BOTH** making a similar ticking sound!

"**I KNOW**" said **MECHNO GIRL**. "**X-BOY**, you need to use your **X-RAY VISION** to see into both cars and find out which one the lion is in. **CHEETECH** you will need to point the camera on the phone towards each car."

So, he did just that. He went up to the first taxi, but the lion **WASN'T THERE!**

Just then, the other taxi started to pull off. So with his **SUPER CHEETAH SPEED**, **CHEETECH** ran up to it and quickly scanned it with the camera on the phone. And there it was! "**IT'S IN THAT ONE**" exclaimed **X-BOY**. So **CHEETECH** was able to stop the driver just in time!

With the lion in-hand, he ran back to the house and climbed up the drainpipe, back into Little Zee's bedroom.

THE SUPER 3 HAD DONE IT!

THEY HAD RESCUED THE LION!

As the problem was now solved, **THE SUPER 3** turned back to normal. And just in time! As Little Zee's mum opened his bedroom door to check on them.

"How's everyone doing?" She asked. "We're all **GREAT**, thanks mum!" Little Zee replied. She gave them all a drink and a gingerbread man, then shut the door behind her.

"**GREAT TEAMWORK!**" Şadé said, as the three of them sat down to play.

CAN YOU GUESS WHAT THEY PLAYED WITH?

That's right! You guessed it! They played with Little Zee's new animal figures.

QUESTION TIME!

 Can you remember the name of the country Little Zee's uncle was visiting from? **FIND THE ANSWER ON PAGE 6.**

 Can you remember what safari animals were in Little Zee's set? **FIND THE ANSWER ON PAGE 14.**

 If you were a Superhero what **SUPER POWERS** would you have used to find the lion?

 Can you draw a picture of yourself using these **SUPER POWERS** to find the lion?

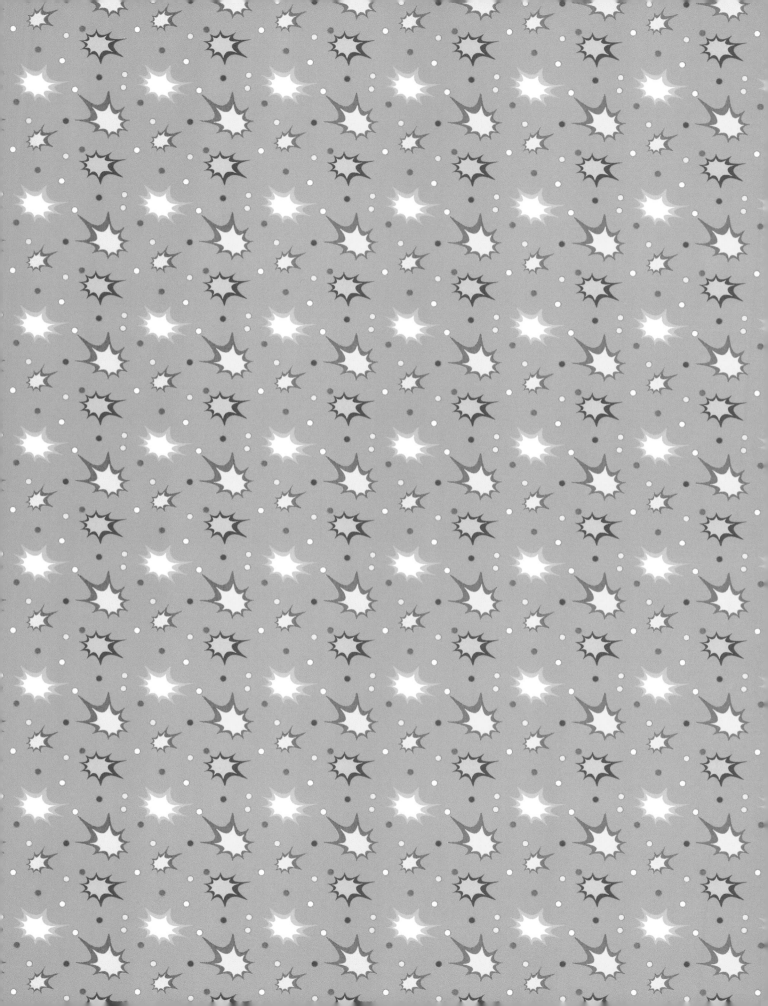

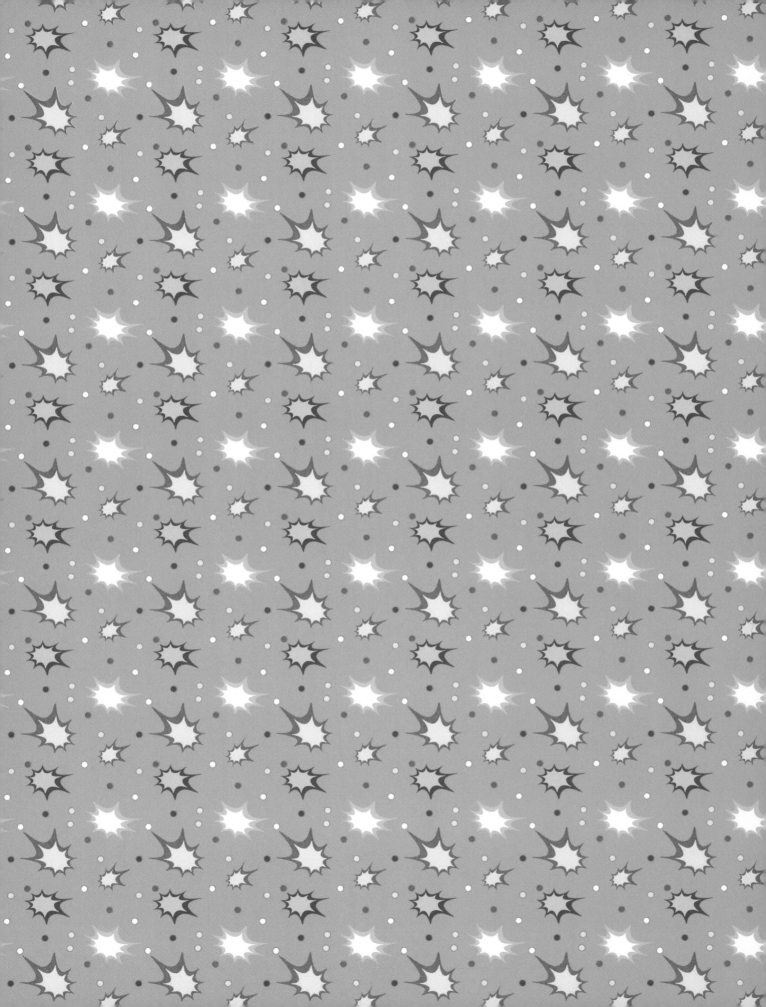

Printed in Great Britain
by Amazon

52499055R00017